Fluberbia

The Rescue!

by

Elizabeth Chapin-Pinotti

LUCKY JENNY PUBLISHING

Published by Lucky Jenny Publishing

Plymouth, California, USA

Copyright © 2012 Elizabeth Chapin-Pinotti
Book design by Ellis Cusses
Illustrations by Elizabeth Chapin-Pinotti

ISBN 978-0615694290

Library of Congress Control Number:

10 05 07 10 12 1

First Edition

To Julia and Claire

They went to the refuge on their way home. They went to the place where the animals roamed. They looked in the gate and the crowd was so sad. Even Ephora thought it was bad.

When the princesses came – earlier that day, they opened the gate – entered right away. But now with their folks, the queen and the king, the gate was all locked. Wrong was something. They looked to their aunt and hoped for a key. After all it was she who should set them all free. She was the one who put them in there. She was the one who before did not care.

Only now she was different,
or so it did seem. Only now she
was nicer, like before was a
dream.

"Auntie Ephora," Princess
Julia called, "before when we
came there was no lock at all."

"All of our new friends , the
animals in there, could come and
could go only they didn't dare."

"Only now the gate's locked," Claire said with a sign.
"We just can't get in. Does anyone know why?"

Ephora
approached the
animals inside.

They all turned
around and
showed their
backsides.

Except for the
lion – who stood
tall and firm.

Who stared
Auntie down –
whose look was
most stern.

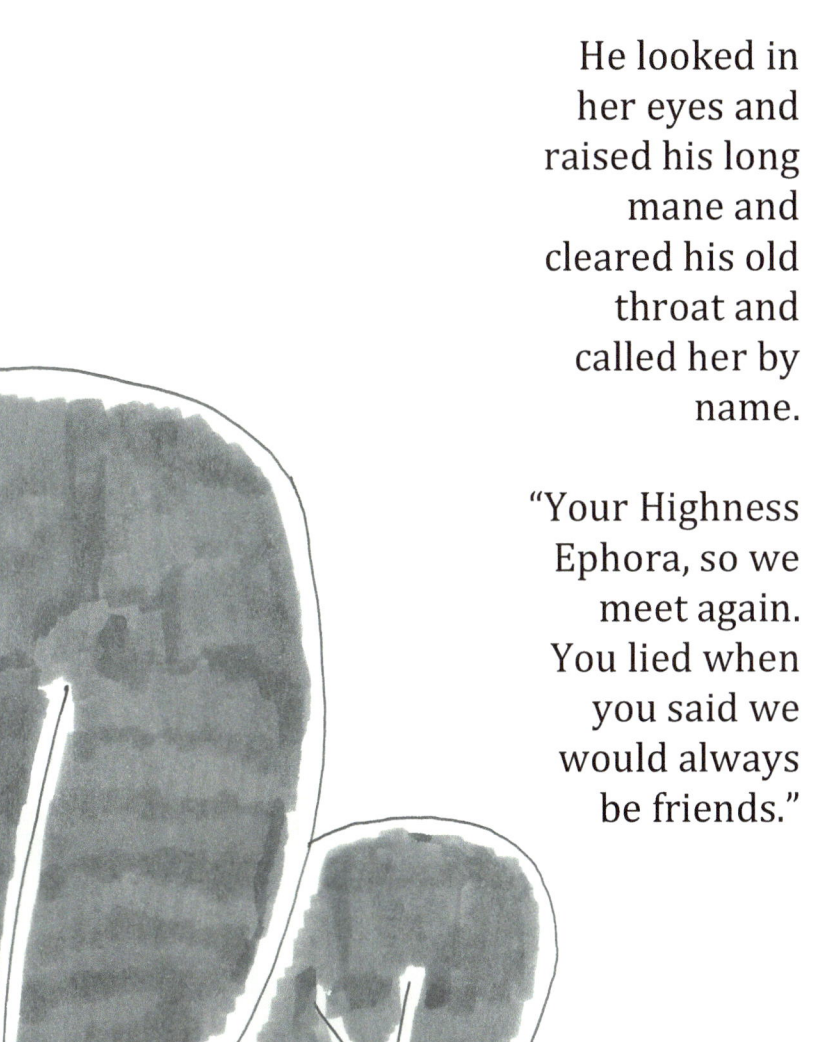

He looked in her eyes and raised his long mane and cleared his old throat and called her by name.

"Your Highness Ephora, so we meet again. You lied when you said we would always be friends."

"You two were once friends – really and truly?
I just can't see it," the twins both said dually.

"Oh, we were great friends," said the animal king.
We ruled all the land. We made lots of bling.
But then I got old and she cast me away
and she brought me to here and it's here I do stay."

13

"We found all the jewels. Told you we'd succeed
And we all came back, like we guaranteed."

"This gate shouldn't lock," said Julia's bright Dad, the King of Fluberbia and he was quite mad. "Ephora you promised. This gate not to lock."

"It was not me. The lock is a shock."

The owl in the back, flew up to the front.
Stood on the gate and spoke out quite blunt,
"When you girls took off – the Cinderbeast roared.

And huffed a big huff – like never before.
"Seems you turned his friend into a big butterfly
and now he is angry – no need to ask why."

The king held his head and gasped in surprise,
"You slayed a strong beast – the sword as your prize?"

"The sword!" cried Ephora. "That's it. That's the way. To open the gate and be on our way."

"Where is it?" said father. The sword from the stone?
I just can't believe you did it alone."

"Where is it, King Lion? Where is the great sword?
We left with a promise and we've kept our word."

"I'm afraid it was stolen," he said sitting down. The beast took it back and he's nowhere around. His best friend you took. Butterflied his mean rump. Used the sword's power – took the jewel from the stump."

"Indeed, that was Claire and our new friend Janie."
"No, no it was Claire. Who pulled the sword free."
Janie, she spoke up. Like she did before.
"But you told me how. We're in debt ever more."

"Well that is just fine," Julia spoke again. "But we need it back to help our new friends."

Claire looked at Julia and then dad and mom. "It's back to the stone – we shouldn't be long."

The brave twins took off – into the forest Enchanted. Into the darkness – fear taken for granted.

They found the pink spot they left in the path.

They followed it to the cinderbeast's wrath. The tunnel of roses was dark and foreboding. Where the beast was they had no way of knowing.

Leaping fast forward – thoughtful steps they did take –
when suddenly the ground – it started to shake.

They looked to the left and they looked to the right.
The sword sat before them surrounded by light.

Julia, she jumped to it and looked right at Claire.
"Sister, it's my turn – you stay right there."

The boulder it sat in – was big and was tall. Julia tugged the handle.   She gave it her all.

"The beast is ferocious," little Claire warned. "With his fire and his fangs he can do you great harm. Give me the sword, I'll fight him off. I did it before. I am really that tough."

"Step back sister dear,"
Julia said shaking.
Loud footsteps
approached – the
ground it was breaking.

The roses above and
the pink path below
both shivered and
shook and moved to
and fro.

The great beast appeared and looked in her eyes and something in them – caught Julia by surprise. She put down the sword .

Claire gasped her chagrin. "What are you doing? You have to beat him."

"He's sad," Julia said and took a step nearer and held out her hand – her fear never fearer!

She stepped forward again, the sword at her side. The fight in her mind, her aunt fought over pride.

"Mr. Beast we are here, to tell you just why – we
needed your friend – as a bright butterfly."
 The beast he stopped smoking – and sat back a bit.
"We saved our parents and he helped with it."

The beast cocked his head and nodded it too.

"See," Julia said sadly, "nothing else we could do."

"We followed a riddle to get back the jewels and your friend the beast – we knew was a tool."

Just then high above, in the tunnel so dark, they heard a small flitter and saw a small spark. The beast he then turned – to the small flying thing – it flew to his hand – and it started to sing!

"I'm still your friend," began his strange verse, "I'm able to fly. It isn't a curse."

Claire moved to Julia and looked at the two. "You speak Fluberbian? What else can you do?"

"A great many things, the butterfly said, "if only you knew us – you'd nothing to dread."

"We've nothing to dread!? You fought us so fierce?"

"And you fought right back and my skin you did pierce. Remember my children, you started the fight. You came to our tunnel and got me in sight. You all just assumed a fight was the way, to solve your great riddle and get on your way."

"But, but," Claire she said.

The beast held up his hand.

"I get that you needed to save your great land.
　　　But you just could have asked. Our roar is quite great,
　　　　　but we are not evil and good friends we do make."

"I'm sorry," said Claire, "that we've caused this strife.
Our cause was quite good, but we've ruined your life."

"Not at all," said the beast – still beastly and big.
"Make me a fly too. Now that I would dig."

The girls shared a glance and smiled to the beast.

And he smiled back – showing big gleaming teeth.

"Just nick his thick skin with the sparkling sword blade and he'll change like me and we'll both have it made."

The beast said again, "I would love to fly too. I'd go see the world – so much I would do. We're stuck in this tunnel – can't leave for the fear we instill in others, but we're really quite dear."

So, Princess Julia did what the beast said.

She pricked his thick skin – right on his big head.

The beast turned to pink, like his friend did before.
And let out one last – loud, fiery roar.
Then in a bright puff – the beast he transformed
and thanked both the girls and flew off in a storm.

Armed with the sword the girls headed back and opened the gate and rescued the pack...
Now the king of the beasts and his fine furry friends Live in Fluberbia and will 'til their end.